Where is My Boaz?

Where is My Boaz?

TEE ASHIRA

iUniverse, Inc.
New York   Bloomington

Where is My Boaz?

iUniverse books may be ordered through booksellers or by contacting:

iUniverse
1663 Liberty Drive
Bloomington, IN 47403
www.iuniverse.com
1-800-Authors (1-800-288-4677)

*Because of the dynamic nature of the Internet, any Web addresses or
links contained in this book may have changed since publication and
may no longer be valid. The views expressed in this work are solely those
of the author and do not necessarily reflect the views of the publisher,
and the publisher hereby disclaims any responsibility for them.*

ISBN: 978-1-4401-1053-5 (sc)
ISBN: 978-1-4401-1054-2 (ebook)

Printed in the United States of America

iUniverse rev. date: 9/11/2009

Thoughts from Tee Ashira

Loving God first and then loving yourself leads you to the pathway toward the man or woman he has prepared for you.

Love is a gift that, if you fail to respect and treasure it, will exit your life.

If you find her, receive her; if you are losing her, fight for her; if you take her for granted, ask her for the hand of forgiveness; and if you have never had her, pray that when she comes, she is whole. Her name is Love.

Our mates are a reflection of who we are. Who are you preparing in the mirror?

To my first Boaz, my Lord and Savior, my father, friend, and redeemer—I can do all things with you. I find safety in your arms, infinity in your touch, and humbleness at your feet.

To my Boaz, my heart, my husband—you are a dream that I never want to awake from. You inspire me to reach new heights in life. You are the very answer to my prayers. Our friendship and love are intoxicated with the power of God.

To my children—you are the essence of God's love for me. I love your spirit, and I am so glad I'm your mother. I love you so much. Never stop loving the Beloved, the most high God.

Introduction

I have met thousands of broken women in the past couple of years, and they all have similar problems—they are single and waiting on a good man or are in a relationship and looking for a better one. The problem with this is that we have to allow the matchmaker himself to do the job. That's God. I can think of a lot of godly men in the Bible who, if they lived in our time, I imagine could have been perfect marriage material.

King David, the second and greatest king over Israel, was a man after God's own heart. His love for God was strong, which would lead me to believe that his love for me would run just as deep. He was a man of strength, evident in the way he slew the Philistines and, of course, in that memorable moment when he slew Goliath. But even in the captivity of his strength, I might have found only temporal happiness because his lustful and adulterous ways would have left me heartbroken.

Peter may have been perfect for me, but I cannot forget that his character vacillated between obstinate resolution and momentary cowardice, as is shown in the story of his denial of his master. Maybe if he were my husband today, we could share moments of passionate lovemaking. He would swear his heart to me at night, but by daylight, before the rooster crowed, he would swear it to another.

Oh yes, did I mention my beloved Solomon, one of the greatest architects who ever lived? He built the temple for God, and a suitable mate in today's society he would have made. He would possess romance, charm, and wisdom, and I would have a house that was fit for *Architectural Digest*. But his passion would burn for everything but God, and a foundation of shallowness with a double-minded man who is unstable in all of his ways is not a firm one.

Okay, now I've got him. Yes, this is it. He's faithful, wealthy, responsible, obedient, and submissive to the will of God for his life and mine. He is a great lover, friend, and father. What else can I say? It's Boaz.

You have to love him; he is the man of every woman's

dreams. Yes, you and I will travel together through his story, so the next time you hear one of your friends say, "Where I can I find a good man?" you can lean over and say, "No, where can I find a Boaz?"

Chapter One

I believe a girl's first true love is her father or the man that God has blessed as a father figure in her life. If that was a void for you, I pray that in the safety of your heavenly father's arms, you are complete.

My father was absent most of my early life, so my grandfather filled that void for me. In his arms as a young child, I felt that safety.

I think that it's crucial that men take time out with their little girls and love them with all their hearts before they look to another for that affection.

It's beautiful to see fathers take their daughters to lunch, pay full attention to their innocent conversations, and tell them of their value. The best gift my grandfather gave me was a grand introduction to the Almighty himself—God. I watched for years as he preached the gospel and raised twelve kids of his own, along with two grandchildren, because of his dedication to his family and his belief that family matters. To this day, he is a hard worker and a loyal husband who submits to the will of God for his life.

He is a Boaz of his time, and that is a blessing because where there lived a Boaz, there lived a Ruth to walk the path with him. Blessings flowed for many generations.

A David and a Devil. I dated early. I would say I was sixteen when I had my first love. I moved out of the house before my time; being a country girl in Mississippi, you long to see independence in some way. Still, I felt I had what it took to finish high school and work, so on the first day of this adventure I met who I thought would be the love of my life. I will change his name so you won't beat him down on the street if you see him because of all the disappointments he delivered.

My grandparents were getting older, and I felt that this independence thing would be great. I got settled in a small place and took a job at a nursing home taking care of the elderly, which left me tired all the time. Taking care of myself was not my focus. My life was full of fast food and late hours of studying.

My grandmother Ruth taught me how to cook at a young age. Her belief is that a woman who doesn't cook may as well break one of the Ten Commandments. So I was on the way home from buying dishes so I could cook and wouldn't commit a major sin

"Where is your help?" he said, and I looked up to see that such a strong voice was coming from a small man. He was not tall but seemed very energetic and truly kind as I watched him carry my boxes up my stairs. His name was David Jackson, a guy I knew from school. I was very surprised to learn that his friend lived in my complex. We started a conversation about school and the people we both knew. That turned into twenty minutes of laughter and a date, which eventually led to a relationship that cost me more than I could afford to pay.

The first couple of weeks were fine. Of course, my folks were unhappy that I was turning seventeen, still in school, and shacking up, which was not smart and never a godly thing to do. Trust that there were prayer meetings about me weekly at home.

I grew to love David. He was handsome and strong, he was my protector, and he was very popular at school. You'd think I had found a man after God's own heart, or at least mine—a man who said he loved God and knew him and would worship him in my presence, quoting scriptures.

So I began to trust him. I adored him regardless of what my family thought; I did it my way. We lived together for one year, and after he graduated, his dreams of success and popularity faded in his eyes. I had thought that he was a man who lived with great zest, but when his dreams did not turn out like he had planned, he felt he had settled. He had dreamed of playing baseball or basketball because he was good at both in high school, but when he had to take a job at a bus station, he just lost hope.

He never confided in me about his family. All I knew was that he lived with his dad, whom I had met several times, and that his dad felt that I was a distraction for David. What could his son have in common with the daughter of a farmer who was a struggling preacher? That was not acceptable in his eyes. David was silent about his mom until, one day, he just got tired of my asking and called her something unspiritual. Red flag, ladies—if a man does not respect his mother, run away. Go and don't stop. It's amazing how God gives us warnings.

Disobedience is painful even when we are out of the will some. God continually waits for that prodigal son or daughter to return to his arms, but we in our own ignorance or stubbornness submit to our will, which is an expensive price for the soul. I was a virgin until

I was seventeen. David was my first except for the sexual molestation I encountered as a child. When sex is forced on a child, I believe that child holds part of his or her virtue because the enemy was planning to steal your innocence but it is God's plan to restore it! But with David, there was no molestation. This was pure will and disobedience to do what I knew was wrong—a bad situation that I made excuses for.

How is it that God can give a command and we give another—a command to do things our way? I was happy to be in what I thought was a healthy relationship. But I did not say it was a godly one. I did not feel pain in the beginning; I felt loved and wanted. Rejection is set in your spirit when your earthly father rejects you or his mother. You want warm arms to hold you tight and make you feel needed in your heart.

The beatings started a year after we settled in together. He started to feel the real pressure of failure in his spirit. This sweet man who I thought was God-sent was the devil in disguise. Makeup ceased to be able to hide the marks that the fist created. Marriage was no longer in my dreams, and neither was college. I could not understand why he was so angry all the time. Was it because he felt he lost his future when his dreams failed?

His father—being a man of prestige—would not

settle for his son being less than what he thought he had molded him to be. But his father contributed to the creation of this monster because he forgot that money does not build character and that divorcing his wife or beating on her because she bored him or was no longer desirable was not the molding his son needed.

David saw his father degrade his mother, and that is what he learned a woman's worth was. So, in essence, he divorced his mother also. He felt the void caused by his mother's absence, and no matter how many different women his dad had around, none were his mom. He always felt alone. I think that when he was older, his mother remarried and had another child, and I think that made him disconnect further from her. She had someone else there who would take his place. But even knowing all of that, he had not lost me. I stayed no matter what. It's amazing to see a man mention God and pray before he beats you, assuming he is a man after God's own heart.

I was in too deep, but I tried to remain there because I felt I had no options. The sounds of my screams would echo in my spirit when a slap across my face left me wounded and sad. I could not go home; I wanted to prove to my grandparents that I could make it and that they were wrong. They decided to move back up to Michigan to retire where my grandfather's parents lived, and I was so sad and alone. I could have left also; they offered, but I wanted to stay.

The next morning, I looked out the window of the apartment we shared with my face battered and my heart broken. My eyes were swollen and tears streamed down my face because I realized that I could be pregnant; I was four weeks late. I had no courage to tell anyone. I prayed that the last beating would relieve me of this child that I could tell was residing in me by the changes in my breasts and the nausea in my belly. Maybe if David kicked me the right way, I would miscarry. But my choices created painful memories for me that I would reflect on later in my life.

I remember it clearly: he walked in the door without speaking to me and dropped his bag. When I asked him where he was going, he threw me to the ground and began to kick me in my side. What I allowed to enter my mind and had hoped for came to pass four hours later, with him nowhere to be found—I lost the child. I cried like a baby alone in the bathroom. Finally, I began to dial his father's number to tell him what had happened.

I will never forget: I explained to this man that he was almost a grandfather and told him of the pain I had endured, saying that if he would just talk to his son… But I got the man that created and molded this demonic force—he hung up on me. The pain you will find when you don't consult with the master of consultants, God, is tremendous. I realized that the grace of God was in my life because not only could David have killed me, I could have caused someone else to be born into this abuse. God is always smarter than we are.

The struggle did not end there. He started to see someone else and would call her from our home. At first I didn't believe it, but it became evident because I saw him less and less. The verbal and emotional abuse continued until the day he put me out of our place and moved this girl in, who happened to deal drugs.

The man that I had known and thought was the greatest turned out to be an abuser, a liar, and a cheater. He had moved on to be a huge drug dealer and had many women. That's how cruel and cold he was. I begged him not to do this, and then he asked me to leave. When I didn't, he threw me out. That's worse than Tyler Perry's *Diary of a Mad Black Woman*—she at least had a ride waiting on her and her clothes packed. I asked him to pray with me, but he told me to pray to him because he was God.

I left all of my belongings behind; all I had were my sweats, my T-shirt, and the Nike shoes that should have left dust in the wind as I got away from this fool. I walked a mile to the pay phone to call my grandparents and ask them to send me a bus ticket. I didn't have to explain; they knew. It was the worst day of my life. I had lost so much, and I still had the nerve to ask God to bring this man back to me. Surely God thought it was a joke.

I got settled at home, where I belonged in the first place, and my folks never said a word. I needed to heal, and even though they never knew exactly what I had been through, they knew I was wounded. Four months passed without hearing from him. I had called and left message after message to see if he would send my things and to inquire about his well-being. I thought he had had enough time to change and that maybe God had heard the prayer I sent up, but I got no reply.

So I called his father, and he told me that David was in prison. I was so startled; I could not believe it. He was sentenced to eight years in prison for trafficking cocaine, he and his new girl. The amazing part was that his father had just left court that day, alone and hurt that his son, the one I was supposedly beneath, was in a jail cell with his new girl and a prostitute who was caught in the car with them when they pulled him over. Of course, that does not sit well with a judge.

God sees all things. Although I had sinned, I was still

a child of the God who puts our enemies beneath us. I did not hang up on David's father that day as he had done to me before. I listened and cried with him and told him God would heal all of his hurts. I sobbed like a baby not because that pain that had left my life was locked up but because my heavenly father made sure I was not there with him. I was protected, and I thank God to this day.

David and I never spoke again. I pray every day that somehow he has come to terms with his demons that have allowed him to cause so much pain in someone else's life. I forgave him, but until I sought God's forgiveness, that relationship haunted me many nights for years.

I still to this day cannot understand my ignorance in what I thought love was. It almost cost me my life. I made a bad choice in not submitting to God's will for my life, and that's to be a virgin until a respectful suitor presented himself to God and then to me. David would have abused our child, so God allowed a miscarriage to save the child and me from that pain. I had made the mistake. Men who are reading this book, run home from work and tell your daughters about their worth. Don't wait until another man supplies a poor substitute for your words. Hold her in your arms and tell her of her value. The pain you will save her later if she has your acceptance now will be more than your heart could take. If you fail her while she is young, it won't matter later when she's older because she will have found what she needs in the enemy's camp.

David Jackson was truly no biblical David. His love for God did not exist because he did not know the God I know. His lust to fulfill his own desires cost him a child and a potential wife. I pray that he was prepared for the punishment that comes from reaping the seeds of hate. As I look back on that relationship, I think that he must have hated women because of the hate he felt for his mother, the first woman in his life. I pray that he has forgiven his mother. I don't know all of the secrets from his father's house, but there were no feminine arms to tuck him in at night and no feminine voice to soothe or nurture his emotions.

There were no tender kisses on his forehead to chase away his pains, and his mother's departure led to my pain and my turmoil. I still will start to cry when I think of that relationship, not because of what I endured but because, even in the midst of my foolishness, the God I love never fails.

I have a son, and I see the importance of loving him deeply. I think the pain from that relationship made me realize that we, as mothers, need to train our boys to have emotions as men, to teach them that it's okay to cry, and to show them how to cherish women because they are queens. They need to understand that every girl and woman is a child of God and of someone else as well. The David in my life didn't understand this. He was no David; he was a devil.

Chapter 2

The Peter Syndrome

I love to read about Peter. The Bible shows that he was a great teacher and a follower of Christ. But he swore his heart to Jesus at night and by day swore it to another. Ladies, please know that if you are with a man who can't keep his word, there is a problem for both of you. It's not that Peter's intentions were not good; he just could not keep his word. And running away was how he failed the most important test in his life.

You hear all the time about teenage girls who get pregnant and the man denies the child is his. You also witness men in relationships, practicing marriage, who later break up with the women because they felt the waters they tested weren't deep enough. I think that the sad part about it all is that most people have not allowed God to do the work in their emotional selves and heal them completely. The first step is seeking God and wanting his help. Step two is loving yourself.

A girlfriend of mine from high school was a tall, swanlike beauty named Anna McDavis. She was destined to be the next Naomi Campbell—she was that beautiful. She dated a famous actor, who I'll refer to as Edwin McCall. He showered her with fancy gifts and trips and vowed that he would be hers forever.

Well, Edwin had the Peter syndrome. Anna had no idea that at the same time he was confessing his undying love to her, he was doing the same thing with his fiancée Nadia.

In 1992, Edwin called Anna to invite her to Jamaica. She invited me to come, and I was so happy. I thought it was amazing that this beautiful model who just happened to be my best friend was dating this famous actor. We were young and exploring our lives. I had always dreamed of exotic vacations and adventurous people, and a true adventure is what we got. When my grandmother was alive, she would tell me that all that glittered was not gold. That is the truth, so help me Jesus.

That trip changed our courses forever. I did not see Edwin much because he had a role in a video shoot there. Anna would see him after work, and I stayed in the hotel overlooking the waters, feeling as if I had died and gone to heaven. That night, he called us to dinner, where we were formally introduced to the real Edwin, who was nothing like what we saw on TV. I formed my own opinion about this man, but I will keep it to myself because you will see it in his fruit. We laughed the whole time about where Anna and I were from, and I knew he had to be the most loyal, faithful mate she would ever find. He adored Anna. Night after night, he would convince me of his love for her. I was so amazed that she had found the love of her life. He was one in a million. After dinner that night, she returned to his room and I returned to mine. I lay there wondering about the good time she had to be having, night after night for a week.

Our flight was scheduled to leave that Sunday morning. It was a beautiful morning, and I hated to leave. Edwin walked us to our car, and we headed to the airport. We were getting ready to board our flight to New York, and I stopped to get some chips and reading material for the plane. Anna and I argued about who would get the magazine on the plane—each of us always wanted to be the first to read fashion magazines or *Jet*—but I was unselfish that day and shared it with her. We were looking at the fashions and talking about some of the models we knew, and then I turned the next page in what seemed like slow motion. As the page turned, we saw Edwin in the magazine with his fiancée, Nadia, who was rumored to be carrying his child. That was the longest flight home.

I know Anna was hurt and embarrassed. She felt the passionate lovemaking that took place in Jamaica was all in vain. I am sure his heart was hers for those moments, but the rooster crowed too quickly. Not long afterward, I moved to Atlanta, and Anna and I lost contact. We went from having conversations once a week to once a year to nothing. I questioned our friendship; we had known each other since junior high, and I was her friend no matter what. But I never got to talk to her about all the trials of her relationship with Edwin. She eventually contacted me later to tell me about those pains and that I owed her four hundred dollars for a three-year old phone bill. I knew that was her way of breaking the silence. After that, we laughed about high school and the people we met through the years, and we simply burst into tears. She told me that she never got over that pain and felt let down. She said that at one time she had been pregnant with his child but lost the baby, and she described how painful that was for her.

I never talked to Anna again. I called the hospital later that week, and they told me she had passed away. I immediately called her modeling agency, and they said she had died of pneumonia. I could not believe what I was hearing. The pain was unbearable, and I felt I needed a lot of answers. My cousin Tim later told me that the rumor back home was that she died of HIV.

I was shaken. This was my best friend; I could not imagine her not ever being tested at all. I often cried and prayed because I know she did not deserve what the heartbreak she got from Mr. Loyalty. It's sad that my friend died of a deadly disease and her "loyal one" moved on with his journey. I can't say where her condition came from, but it's just like when Jesus was being led to the cross—Peter was nowhere to be found even though he promised loyalty. I often wonder, as my best friend lied there covered in her illness, whatever it was, where was her Peter who had sworn his love and loyalty? Where was his friendship? Sometimes we don't realize the degree of our betrayal until the one we swore our love to gets crucified spiritually and emotionally.

Chapter 3

Solomon or Solo

Years passed, and I was persuaded to waitress at a club with my best friend Sara Weiss while I was going to school. Sara and I would go out on the weekends and do what girls do, and that was basically nothing. One weekend, we went to her cousin's barbecue party, and as I walked in I felt a tug on my arm. I looked up to see a tall gent with eyes full of hope. His name was Rodney Harp, and he was a successful professional. With my first look at him, I knew we had a connection. I was nineteen, young and immature; I'm sure Bozo would have been charming too. In other words, a person who can make me laugh and has patented charm will get me every time. No offense to Rodney—he was sweet, wealthy, and spoiled. He had a smile that would melt ice and a face that made *GQ* models seem average.

Rodney was a man's man—at least, that's what I thought at the time. My definition of that was a man who was at the top of his game and in control of his career, his finances, and his future, but what I admired the most about Rodney was his wisdom. He lived in Texas, so we exchanged numbers and kept in touch for months.

My definition of a real man today is a man who is focused on God and who knows that through his obedience, the other luxuries of life shall be added.

Sara convinced me to take a trip with her to Houston one weekend to see her boyfriend. I remember calling my grandfather to let him know, and he told me to slow down, concentrate on college, and really start to focus on what God's purpose for my life was. But I thought I had all the answers and once again did not need God's assistance.

It costs to be the boss. I really needed to heal after David, and I became friends with a guy who attended my church. It was nothing more than a friendship; he knew that I had only been intimate with one person in my life and that I wanted to be married before I traveled down that road again. So our friendship was born even as I traveled freely into the arms of another. This will sound like a true love story like the book of Solomon, a story saturated with sexual escapades. The message the world sends today is that freedom, perversion, and premarital sex are natural and commitment is old-fashioned.

God created sex, and it was good. In today's society, love is now lust, and lasting commitment is an itch with no strings attached. What am I saying in all of this? Relationships are not valued. We freely do what we want with whom we want without first evaluating the consequences. Well, that weekend, I never asked Rodney about his relationship with God. I made an assumption based on his mild manners and soft undertone that he had to know God.

People, just because a man or woman is quiet during the first couple of weeks of romancing you, it doesn't mean that he or she knows God or is a meek person. I called Rodney when I arrived in Houston, and that night he, some friends, and I later went to breakfast and had a good time. It amazes me how people portray what they want you to see and reveal later who they really are. He took me safely back to the hotel where I was staying, looked me in my eyes, and said I was all he would ever need and that he wanted to have a serious relationship. Houston was just a couple of hours from Atlanta by plane, so we would see each other often. We would go have dinner and hang out when he came to town, and I was starting to believe he was right for me. We had a mutual friend named Fred Jones who tried to keep us together—or shall I say apart. We were well informed of each other's activities when we were apart by the Judas-like betrayer. Rodney paid Fred well to come to Atlanta, spy on me, and report back on what my activities were. I had reconnected with my God, and life was moving along well for me. I felt that I was in a good place, and I did not want to mess that up. When Rodney was away, he would call me every day and we would chat for hours about our lives, careers, and the strong connection we had. It was undeniably strong. I thought at the age of nineteen that this was the one—we were so right for each other. He was the man I would marry. Young women, the devil reels you in to think a relationship could lead to the altar, but he takes you on dangerous detours. Rodney was twenty-five and very experienced.

But when we were apart, we missed each other, and when we were together, we could not get enough. We were friends, and I have always thought that was so important in a relationship. But we wanted to see each other more. For seven months I stayed in Atlanta, thinking from time to time of moving to Texas. I was either bold or crazy, but I did it. Rodney wanted me there, and surely it showed. But how crazy was it to travel with no guidance at all? He offered to move me there and pay for my place while

I finished school. Did I ask God about this venture? No, but trust me—I would call on him later.

I arrived in this city of dreams with my heart on the line and my eyes on Rodney, who was waiting for me there to show me his huge world filled with affection and tenderness and all of this wisdom, along with riches and calamity. He was my Solomon, and I was one of his many brides. He always made time for me, no matter what. I never had to ask him to do anything for me; he would just do it. The advice he would give me showed wisdom beyond his years, but I often wondered whether he counseled himself. I was provided for emotionally and financially, my love was refreshing, and the miles I traveled proved that. Someone please tell me why I was not informed. Oh yes, I forgot—I didn't ask, but hail to King Rodney!

Months after I arrived, a young woman showed up at the door in tears. She explained to me that she had followed Rodney to my house and introduced herself as the mother of his daughter. My heart was shattered. I could not confront him on this. I was so hurt that he left the mother of his child to be with me. The problem was that the mother didn't know it; Rodney's ex told me there were many other women. I could not stay in a relationship knowing that I shared the love of my life with other women, and I could not ignore the fact he had a child here. So I was on my way out the door with no money. I would have to go back to Atlanta and start again, but I did what I had to do.

In my heart, it hurt to leave, but as a woman I deserved more than that. The best part about the situation was that we never slept together. We were to become engaged the week before my surprise visit; we even shopped for rings. But it was over. I walked away but not without a broken spirit, heart, and soul. You see, again without the instructions of God, I was led into another trap of the enemy. Later I would repent—true repentance, meaning that I could not bear that cross again. I could not keep making these types of choices and then call on God to bail me out.

I think I could have called on him in the beginning and saved myself a lot of heartache. I left my Solomon and was solo, but not without pain and consequences.

Oh daughters of Jerusalem, please do not awaken love before it is time; let it sleep.

Chapter 4

Ruth's Transformation

Close your eyes and try to imagine the love of your life—the one who has claimed you—dying suddenly. No matter the explanation for his death, you are unprepared.

Ruth was born and raised in Moab, and the Moabites worshipped a God by the name of Chemosh. Their form of worship included the sacrifice of children to Chemosh as an offering. (See 2 Kings 3:27). The people were idol worshippers, and on top of everything, Moab was a cursed place. Centuries before, Abraham's nephew had left Sodom and Gomorrah with his two daughters and escaped destruction by fire and brimstone. The daughters, whose mother had been turned into a pillar of salt as punishment for her disobedience, felt alone and felt that they and their father were the only three people on the entire earth. They got their father drunk on two consecutive nights, and they each had sex with him and became pregnant. One of the children resulting from the incest was named Moab, and his descendants were the Moabites. Because of this great sin, the nation he produced became accursed.

Can you imagine what it must have been like for Ruth to grow up in a place like Moab? No laughter, no praise, no God. She was so different from the man she married. Her husband's name was Kilion, the son of Elimelech and Naomi. Kilion, whose name means "unhealthy," must have brought some sort of pains to their relationship. His vows would not be broken by his choice but by God's.

I see a lot of myself in Ruth, although my story is the opposite of this one because I grew up in a Christian home where my grandfather was a minister and where I was taught to pray for the husband that God would put in my life. God was the director, and we were the choir.

My husband was a believer before I married him, when I was twenty-two. We were equally yoked. I had broken that pattern of bad choices and did it the right way—at least I thought I had. After we got married, we got settled but realized we were different in so many ways. Emotionally and spiritually, we were like water and oil.

I tried to make it work as hard as I could, and in my heart I know that he did too, but it was over before it started, it seems. Seven years drifted away because of my decision not to take my time and get to know him first.

We were married within five months of meeting and did not have the proper counseling. I thought it was better to marry than burn. Don't get me wrong— there were many good days in our marriage. My children are a part of that, but I know now in my heart that if I had trusted God and allowed myself to mature spiritually and heal completely, I would have saved us both a lot of pain.

My husband did not die as Ruth's did; he walked away. Where there is a lack of faith, there is no God. Where there is no God, there is no foundation. And if there is no healing in your heart from your past, there is no future. After seven years, my marriage was over. Unlike Ruth, I had two children, but I still was alone.

It is impossible for a man to give you what he is not taught to give. It starts with the mother. And it is impossible for a woman to do the same if she cannot submit to authority, which starts with the father. I want you to understand the love and respect that I have and will always have for this man because he is one of the most beautiful people I know and a great father to our children. He did not walk away because he was a bad person. He walked away because he spent seven years trying to repair my broken spirit and heal my pain, and he was not whole himself. He did not allow God to do his job, which is to be my savior, and I could not carry the pains of yesterday that would keep me from my tomorrow.

Just as Ruth transformed her pain to faithfulness to Naomi's God, my God had never left the throne regardless of the pain and the heartache. He is a God that restores, and the death of my marriage built my character and put me on the pathway to my future. It was not my fault. I did not walk away—he did. I stayed faithful. I sowed seeds, and as I continued in my praise, I prayed that God would remember my sacrifice and my tears and would send me a man after his own heart to walk this course with me. Although Ruth had encountered death, in a way that is no different than a man walking away. A death of a covenant takes place when marital vows are broken. So you go through the emotions of that loss, and you open up that casket and put in that rejection, the pain, and the tears to be buried. It is indeed a painful process that can leave you bitter. But as Ruth and I did, allow God to make the transformation in your heart and arise from these emotions. Tomorrow is a new day.

Chapter 5

Boaz the Man

Now let's talk about Boaz. Heroes are easier to admire than define. In his dealings with people, he was always sensitive to their needs. He was not consumed with himself; his employees, relatives, and others were colored with kindness.

He did things the right way; he was a man of order and a man of his word. He had a keen sense of responsibility and was a brilliant lawyer and a successful and shrewd businessman. He had an awareness of his choices, and he was wealthy. His obedience to God outweighed his obedience to himself.

But putting his great characteristics aside, you have to know where he came from to understand this man. Boaz came from the womb of Rahab, a prostitute from Jericho. (You can find her story in Joshua 2:1, Matthew 1:5, Hebrews 11:31, and James 2:25.) Her profession could have exposed her to diseases from men who used her for one purpose only. How could a man with such great strength and integrity have a mother who was a whore?

Imagine him at dinner with his future fiancée talking about his family tree, describing his mother—a liar, a traitor to her nation, and, most embarrassing, a woman of the night. Let's be honest; today we would judge her for her profession. Some modern commentators suggest that she was a cult prostitute who plied her trade in the temples of Canaanite gods. When Josephus wrote his twenty-volume history of the Jews back in the first century, he substituted the word *innkeeper* for *harlot* when he wrote about Rahab.

Boaz's mother was a survivor. She harbored spies that Joshua sent from the Israeli camp to check out Jericho. We might think that Rahab, being a Canaanite and a prostitute, would never be interested in God. Yet she was willing to risk everything on a God she barely knew. I find it unfair that we judge a person solely on her background or lifestyle. Rahab showed faith that would later bring her great honor. I think the designation of harlot heightens the grace of God.

Boaz had an encounter at school or church with a person who would remind him about her past. Can you see the people laughing, whispering about his mother, not knowing or caring that God had brought her into a new place?

She was a wife, mother, and worshipper, and she was redeemed. Her past was behind her. But surely people spread rumors when they learned that the woman Boaz loved and cherished the most, his mother, had a shameful past full of deep, dark secrets.

I can see him in the middle of the night, crying himself to sleep because his friends were cruel, taunting him about rumors they heard from their parents. He would be holding his favorite pillow as the tears rolled down his cheek and the thoughts of the trail of men that had left his mother's bed would not stop. This saddens and penetrates his broken spirit because the pain he feels is not his fault. It stems from the past of his mother and some bad choices she once made.

I think of my son being older and walking into a bookstore to find his mother's novels, learning that there were abuse, other children, and rejection in her life. I imagine the tears that would fall in disbelief that the woman who in his eyes was perfect, the love of his life, was not always whole. But seeing the woman that God destined her to be would overtake any pain that he might feel. Perhaps Rahab's naming her son Boaz, which means "strength," was prophetic because she knew the trials that he would face. As he grew older and became a man, he allowed those tears to be buried where they fell and could finally look into his mother's eyes and see what she had become instead of what she used to be.

God had prepared Boaz for greatness. Later in life, he could see beyond Ruth's sorrow and her past and see her greatness and her redeemer.

Chapter 6

I want to walk with you through the course of Ruth and Boaz's meeting. To me, this is the most amazing love story that I have ever read. The verses quoted here are from Chapter 2 of the Book of Ruth in the New Living Translation (NLT).

Verse 5: "Then Boaz asked his foreman, 'Who is that woman over there?'"

Boaz is taking notice of her.

Verse 8: "Boaz went over and said to Ruth, 'Listen, my daughter. Stay right here with us when you gather grain; do not go to any other fields. Stay right behind the young women working in my field."

Verse 10: "Ruth fell at his feet and thanked him warmly. 'What have I done to deserve such kindness?' she asked. 'I am only a foreigner.'"

It's obvious in these scriptures that these two have officially been introduced and have taken special notice of each other. Both were simply executing the plan of God and being themselves.

Verse 13: "'I hope I continue to please you, sir,' she replied. 'You have comforted me by speaking so kindly to me, even though I am not one your workers.'"

In the King James Version, Ruth says, "Let me find favour in thy sight, my lord." In expressing her appreciation for his kindness, Ruth addresses Boaz as "my lord." Ladies, this demonstrates not only Ruth's obedience for authority but also her respect for it.

She was prepared for this meeting. Although it was ordained by God, she still showed consistence in her virtue. She was honoring her husband before she knew him, and Boaz was respecting his wife before he knew her. I believe the right man gives his right woman that respect. She is highly favored in his eyes.

Verse 14 (NLT): "At mealtime Boaz called to her, 'Come over here, and help yourself to some food. You can dip your bread in the sour wine.' So she sat with his harvesters, and Boaz gave her some roasted grain to eat." This was the perfect invitation by Boaz for Ruth to sit with him. Where people were seated at this time followed protocol, and here it also followed God's desired plan. Her man is requesting her presence near him at the table and showing her the utmost respect by promoting her from the most humble circumstances.

Ruth was no longer an unknown peasant but a special dinner guest of Boaz, the owner of the estate. Boaz was no longer an isolated rich man but a gracious host with love for a recipient of the grace of God. This was no longer an impersonal relationship; Ruth became recognized in his eyes and those of others as a very special person. She had been honored by the head of the estate.

This is the divine plan of the master planner himself. Ruth, a Moabite girl who was considered a peasant, was invited to eat with a Jewish aristocrat.

Boaz was practicing hospitality (Heb. 13:2), but he was also pursuing a personal love relationship. In the plan of God, personal love may be so strong that it knocks a person to the ground. A man will find himself doing things that he has never done. The meal was provided to Ruth compliments of logistical grace. The hospitality Boaz showed was free of racial discrimination, protocol seating, grace, promotion, and personal love—the perfect introduction at the perfect place at the perfect time. All of this is evidence that it was God's plan.

Here, Boaz showed his protection for Ruth; I am sure he did not allow any sexual harassment from the male hired hands. Being a damsel, she was a young and very attractive Moabite girl, but being a peasant, she faced scolding, discipline, and other types of harassment. Boaz addressed these things before they even became an issue by establishing the scope of her job. She was allowed to glean even among the sheaves, which was not commonly permitted. She was not to be disciplined by the hired hands, and she had a light workload because the boss had already ordered that the other workers purposely pull out some grain for her.

You go, boy! Men, are you getting this? This is powerful. Boaz is simply closing the door to the enemy by taking care of his wife-to-be, protecting her from any other types of abuse or mishaps that might come her way. He is taking his leadership role from physical to spiritual. He is making sure she has all that she needs, providing for her. Love your wife now if you have her to love. But if you are single, nurture her in the spirit so you can be prepared when she enters your life at the perfect place and perfect time.

Seven and Completion

According to Israel's calendar, the harvest fest started with the feast of first fruits, which was the first day after the Passover. The barley harvest was followed by the wheat harvest and then the Pentecost. The Passover fell approximately on the first week of April, and the Pentecost fell fifty days later, which would take it into June. So Ruth labored in Boaz's fields no more than fifty days, roughly seven weeks. At the end of the harvest, Ruth was no longer working in Boaz's fields. They were separated and did not see each other like they had before.

Men, imagine that the woman who has just turned your world upside down emotionally with butterflies of love leaves. You went from seeing her every day to not seeing her at all. When you saw her heart was complete, you wanted to take care of her emotionally, physically, and mentally. And the crazy part of it all was that you didn't know why.

The Threshing Floor and the Redeemer

Ruth, Chapter 3, Verses 1–6 (New Living Translation):

> One day Naomi said to Ruth, "My daughter, it's time that I found a permanent home for you, so that you will be provided for. Boaz

is a close relative of ours, and he's been very kind by letting you gather grain with his young women. Tonight he will be winnowing barley at the threshing floor. Now do as I tell you—take a bath and put on perfume and dress in your nicest clothes. Then go to the threshing floor, but don't let Boaz see you until he has finished eating and drinking. Be sure to notice where he lies down; then go and uncover his feet and lie down there. He will tell you what to do." "I will do everything you say," Ruth replied. So she went down to the threshing floor that night and followed the instructions of her mother-in-law.

Notice the three things that Naomi told Ruth to do: wash, annoint, and clothe herself.

Verses 7–14:

After Boaz had finished his meal and was in good spirits, he lay down beside the heap of grain and went to sleep. Then Ruth came quietly, uncovered his feet, and lay down. Around midnight, Boaz suddenly woke up and turned over. He was surprised to see a woman lying at his feet! "Who are you?" he demanded. "I am your servant Ruth," she replied. "Spread the corner of your covering over me, for you are my family redeemer." "The Lord bless you, my daughter!" Boaz exclaimed. "You are showing even more loyalty now than you did before, for you have not gone after a younger man, whether rich or poor. Now don't worry about a thing, my daughter. I will do what is necessary, for everyone in town knows you are a virtuous woman. But while it is true that I am one of your family redeemers, there is another man who is more closely related to you than I am. Stay here tonight, and in the morning I will talk to him. If he is willing to redeem you, very well. Let him marry you. But if he is not willing, then as surely as the Lord lives, I will redeem you myself! Now lie down here until morning." So Ruth lay at Boaz's feet until morning, but she got up before it was light enough for people to recognize each other. For Boaz had said, "No one must know that a woman was here at the threshing floor."

Notice in this that when Naomi told Ruth to clothe and perfume herself, it was to prepare herself for her redeemer. Naomi's advice to her daughter-in-law is debated strongly among theologians. It has been suggested that Naomi was sending Ruth to the threshing floor to have sex with Boaz or to seduce him in some way.

But I believe that this was just part of the execution of God's plan and of the process of their premarital engagement. In Ezekiel 16:8–10, the Lord spoke to Ezekiel concerning Jerusalem, speaking symbolically of Jerusalem as a wife:

> And when I passed by you again, you were old enough to be married. So I wrapped my cloak around you to cover your nakedness and declared my marriage vows. Then I bathed you and washed off your blood, and I rubbed fragrant oils in your skin. I gave you expensive clothing of linen and silk, embroidered, and sandals made of fine leather.

This description of God's marital process with Jerusalem was in the same divine order as setting the marriage canopy and the attendant intimacy. Naomi's plan was clearly geared to bring about both intimacy and, ultimately, the marriage of Boaz and Ruth.

God's marital vows to us were in this same order. He washed us when we were covered in sin; when we were rejected by others, he cleaned us up with his cloth of mercy. Then he anointed us with his oil of the Holy Spirit, clothed us in his love and righteousness, and gave us his unfailing covenant.

He made us his bride. Women, there is a process that must take place, I believe, before we go to the threshing floor and meet our Boaz. The preparation begins when we allow God's love to penetrate us and become his bride by following the guidelines he has set for us, which specify that we are to be married to him first. When Ruth told Boaz, "Spread the corner of your covering over me because you are my family redeemer," she was saying to him, Protect me and cover me from all the pains of my past, all the heartbreaks that I have had, the losses that have left me paralyzed through the years, and the tiredness of my journey because you are my redeemer.

If your Boaz has not entered your life and you don't feel that you have that protection, God confirms in Ezekiel 16:8 that he will cover your nakedness from all the pains of the molestations and the rejections from the men who have raped you physically, mentally, and emotionally. With his cloak, he will declare his marriage vows to you and make you his wife.

Boaz was covering his bride. He would tell her later in the scripture not to worry about a thing because he would do what was necessary to make her an honorable woman although there was another man closer than he who could marry her. He put his woman's heart at ease as he leaned over and whispered in her ear, If all else fails and he doesn't want you, I do. That's the same thing the master says: When all fails you, I will be your redeemer. I want you.

Threshing floors were nothing more than level places of smooth rock or pounded earth located on a hill, where the grain could be separated from the chaff by tossing the threshed grain into the wind that rose in the evening from the Mediterranean. The grain, heavier, fell to the ground as the chaff was blown away.

Ruth did not deviate from the plan of God to seek youth or the love of money, two worldly desires. The master of all courts, God Almighty himself, had already approved the marriage of Ruth and Boaz. The courts of the land had not caught up; it was arranged by divine appointment. Ruth obeyed Boaz submissively, but he did not demand that she do what he told her to do. They were a system; they were already one.

The Separation

Sometimes, relationships encounter a separation period, during which one person goes out of town for weeks on business or for some other reason, and both partners have time to think about the relationship. For Boaz, surely by this time doubt had set in about Ruth and the future of the relationship. Do I love her? Does she love me? Can I make her happy? Perhaps he analyzed the age difference between them.

This is anguish to the soul because these rationalities are the symptoms of being lovesick. Surely Boaz and Ruth were thinking of each other daily. Ruth had to wonder whether he found her attractive and whether, because of her past as a Moabite, she was worthy of having a man like Boaz to love her.

Our gifts from God are not packaged the way we would like sometimes, but that doesn't mean that they are not gifts. After Ruth and Boaz had completed the phase of attraction, they journeyed through the stages of separation. This is a true test in any relationship.

The duration of the separation was no longer than seven weeks because it ended when Ruth met Boaz at the threshing floor. The number seven is a powerful and symbolic number in the Bible, often symbolizing completion.

Spiritual Rapport

Ruth 3:10 says, "'The Lord bless you my daughter!' Boaz exclaimed. 'You are showing more family loyalty now than you did before, for you have not gone after a younger man, whether rich or poor.'" Spiritual rapport is important for many reasons. With spiritual rapport, physical differences such as race are overcome because the issues are spiritual, not temporal.

In return for her loyalty, Boaz recognized Ruth's virtue and values. She was motivated by the love of God. Although she was not yet in spiritual maturity because of her nation's customs, she was receiving a divine blessing and was motivated to love the Lord and obey his commandments. She validated that loyalty and love through her loyalty and caring for Naomi and the desire to serve Naomi's God.

That night on the threshing floor, Boaz told Ruth to lie down and go to sleep, clearly implying that she should sleep with him. He did not send her away. Whether sleeping with Boaz the rest of the night included sex it not clear, though it is within the realm of possibility.

The question has been asked, Did they sleep together before they had a legal right? The answer is no because what they did was to fulfill the plan of God. It was right because Boaz was her destiny. In the case of Ruth and Boaz, the temporal relationship had not been instantiated when the spiritual relationship became operational. Such is the nature of spiritual rapport, as well as faith. The spiritual precedes the temporal.

The Lord is the ultimate judge of marital issues (Heb. 13:4). The doctrinal believer acts on the spiritual before the temporal. When Boaz tells Ruth to lie down and go to sleep, he is clearly exercising authority. This command does not mean that she should have sex with him here because sex does not involve authority. Women may initiate love or even a request for sex, but such a request does not come from authority. It simply comes from love.

They were wrapped in the same cloak together. He was the leader, she was the follower, and they were both blessed because they were obeying the plan of God. They were walking in their purpose. They were operating in the spiritual and left the rest of the establishment to catch up. Notice that Boaz not only protected Ruth by providing for her, he also respected her reputation. He told Ruth that no one must know that a woman was here at the threshing floor because women who went to the threshing floor were usually prostitutes. If people knew that Ruth's relationship started like the relationship of a harlot, Ruth's reputation as a woman of virtue would be ruined. I love that Boaz is so concerned about his woman's virtue that he protects it at all cost.

Verse 15 tells us more of the story: "Then Boaz said to her, 'Bring your cloak and spread it out.' He measured out six scoops of barley into her cloak and placed it on her back. Then he returned to the town." My Christian brothers and sisters, understand that this man is operating in the manner of Christ Jesus himself. This woman came for her redeemer and left with redemption and restoration.

Patience Is Virtue

Ruth and Boaz did not marry right away because of the legal issue concerning the other kinsman. After the meeting at the threshing floor, Ruth returned to Naomi with barley and a promise.

Ruth 3:18 says, "Then Naomi said to her, 'Just be patient, my daughter, until we hear what happens. The man won't rest until he settles things today." Naomi is simply telling Ruth to sit still, to rest in faith.

There is nothing that Ruth can do to solve the legal issue. It's in the Lord's hands, and she must wait for him to solve it. She must wait in faith on a promise from a man that she has trusted and a God she cannot see.

She could have taken matters into her own hands by manipulating the situation, perhaps meeting with the other kinsman and talking with him. But that was not the way it was predestined to be. She waited in faith and did not walk ahead of God's plan. Even though she could not solve the legal issue, she could have walked before God, doing it her way and jeopardizing the situation. The mature believer knows when to act and when to wait. I think we need to understand that we cannot ask God for a Boaz and then get impatient and try to help him out. We need to understand that Ruth had faith. She believed her man's word; he said that he would handle it, and she had to wait patiently as he acted.

I need the women who are married to understand this: when your Boaz at home tells you that he has the situation under control, you need to rest in faith. If you have prayed about the situation and practiced faith, then it will be taken care of. God will allow your Boaz to handle the situation.

I saw a movie recently by the talented Tyler Perry. In one scene, a man tells his love that all she has to do is wake up in the morning and he would handle the rest. He wanted his woman to have faith in him to trust that he wanted to provide everything she needed; all she had to do was wake up.

Ladies, I know that we live in a time when we can

handle things ourselves. We often foolishly take on the role of Eve and bring death to the relationship by not trusting the man that God has put in authority over us. If you are single and waiting on a Boaz, realize that you were not there to assist the Almighty in the construction of the universe, so why would he need your guidance on constructing your Boaz? He has your back. Patience is virtue. Ruth understood that. God is speaking to the ladies who are anxious, saying softly, All you have to do is wake up in the morning and trust me because I've got you. Boaz has arrived.

Ruth 4:1–4

> So Boaz went to the town gate and took a seat there. When the family redeemer he had mentioned came by, Boaz called out to him, "Come over here, friend. I want to talk to you." So they sat down together. Then Boaz called ten leaders from the town and asked them to sit as witnesses. And Boaz said to the family redeemer, "You know Naomi, who came back from Moab? She is selling the land that belonged to our relative Elimelech. I felt that I should speak to you about it so that you can redeem it if you wish. If you want the land, then buy it here in the presence of these witnesses. But if you don't want it, let me know right away, because I'll redeem it.

Can you see Boaz taking a deep breath here? He is simply going through the legal process that is required for the land, but in his heart he knows that the discussion is about his woman. He is a shrewd businessman; watch him in action.

Ruth 4:5–11

> Then Boaz told him, "Of course, your purchase of the land from Naomi also requires that you marry Ruth, the Moabite widow. That way, she can have children who will carry on her husband's name and keep the land in the family. "Then I can't redeem it," the family redeemer replied, "because this might endanger my own estate. You redeem the land; I cannot do it." Now in those days it was the custom in Israel for anyone transferring a right of purchase to remove his sandal and hand it to the other party. This publicly validated the transaction. So the other family redeemer drew off his sandal as he said to Boaz, "You buy the land." Then Boaz said to the elders and to the crowd standing around, "You are witnesses that today I have bought from Naomi all the property of Elimelech, Kilion, and Mahlon. And with the land I have acquired Ruth, the Moabite widow of Mahlon, to be my wife. This way she can have a son to carry on the

name of her dead husband and inherit the family property here in his hometown. You all are witnesses today."

Wow. The land sounded good to the redeemer, but he felt that the baggage that came along with it was too much to handle, so he was out for the count. He threw in his sandal and ran for his life. He told Boaz he could have it because it was too much responsibility for him. I understand that even though I am making this sound funny, it is painful to think that men may want the beauty that a wife brings but not be willing to take the baggage of her past, including the children she has, the husband who died, or the affairs of the heart she knew before him. Some men want the girlfriend and the benefits of a wife but do not want the responsibility of making the relationship too serious for them and providing her with that covenant.

The redeemer rejected the right of redemption on the grounds that it would mar his own estate. *Mar* means "devalue" or "corrupt," so the point the redeemer was making was that that if he bought the field, it would very shortly go to the son of Ruth. If he could have simply bought the field, it would have simply added to his own estate. But if he had to buy it and then give it away to the son of Ruth, then the net present value of the field would not be adequate to cover his initial investment.

If Ruth had a son within a year, the redeemer could have not made enough from the field to cover his investment. There was also the fact that if he gave Ruth a child, his own son would not be heir to the estate. But whatever the reason, from his monetary perspective, Ruth wasn't worth it. Boaz, however, did not see it that way, He saw Ruth as someone more valuable than all the money in the world. His obedience was to God and not himself. Boaz, a Hebrew name that means "strength," was strong enough to handle the whole package. He wasn't about to walk away from his woman because she was a poor business investment. He wanted her in the beginning; even before he started the negotiation of the deal, he saw her value and her worth. Men of weakness, by all means throw in your sandals and run for your very lives. Your gift may not come packaged the way that you would like it to be; it might arrive abused, mistreated, scorn, hurt, and full of baggage, and this job may not be for you. So move over, because Boaz has arrived or soon will.

The Wedding Day

Ruth 4:11–13

> Then the leaders and all the people standing in the gate replied, "We are witnesses! May the Lord make the woman who is coming into your home like Rachel and Leah, from

whom all the nation of Israel descended! May you prosper in Ephrathah and be famous in Bethlehem. And may the Lord give you descendants by this young woman who will be like those of our ancestor Perez, the son of Tamar and Judah."

So Boaz married Ruth and took her home to live with him. When he slept with her, the Lord enabled her to become pregnant, and she gave birth to a son.

Ruth 4:17: "And they named him Obed. He became the grandfather of Jesse and the grandfather of David."

After a drama at the city gate where court was held, Boaz, the most eligible bachelor in town, had married a Moabite girl who was a widow in poverty and had no place to call home. The purpose and the will of God was celebrated that day. The whole town was there to witness it except for Ruth and Naomi, who were still at home waiting on a promise and showing faith in God.

The ceremony was over before the afternoon; it had all started that day when Boaz awoke with Ruth lying near him on the threshing floor and had heightened to a marriage before noon. When Boaz went to claim his woman, she was waiting in faith. Can you see her eyes tear up as her baby walks through the door with the crowd behind him? Ruth had waited patiently for God and her man to fulfill his promise and had faith in both of them, and she knew that they would deliver. Ruth waited by the window, knowing this battle was not hers but the Lord's.

She was rejoicing with the happiness of a recipient of the love and grace of God; she got her man. The wedding and the honeymoon were taking place before she knew it. The next thing she knew, Ruth was pregnant. The Lord enabled her conception, and she gave birth to a son. The past was gone. The redeemer, God himself, sought a man for Ruth who would fulfill this great honor. Men before Boaz might not have seen Ruth's value, but God found a man who did, and, oh, what a beautiful wedding day.

Boaz is perhaps the greatest husband in the Bible because he was spiritually mature and the recipient of the blessings of God. He was the tree planted by the gardens that brought forth fruit in its season. The only great biblical marriage that compares to the marriage of Boaz and Ruth is that of Abraham and Sarah.

But whereas Abraham and Sarah got married before they reached spiritual maturity, Boaz and Ruth did not marry until Boaz reached spiritual maturity. I think you could agree that Boaz's preparation began long before Ruth arrived, with his mother Rahab.

This is the kind of love that a man has for his mother, no matter where her fault lies. He understood that she might have been imperfect in her past, but through God's mercy she was made whole. Boaz was groomed as a child through the pain he endured, and he did not allow his mother's past to affect his life in a negative way.

He showed that same love for Ruth. He did not see her past; he saw her future and saw himself in it. That is the maturity that only a man who is spiritually connected with God can have. A lot of men cannot let go of their mothers' mistakes and somehow carry that bitterness with them into their future relationships. Because they feel the first love of their lives failed them, they cannot have success with any other women. But allowing God to heal that innermost hurting part of your past, no matter who hurt you, can bring you to the place of spiritual maturity and make you that Boaz that you are predestined to be. And then you can look at the love of your life, whether it is your mother or your wife, and you can see what she has become instead of what she was.

Knowing Your Ruth

At first glance, we might have thought the marriage of Ruth and Boaz would not be a match made in heaven. Some may say they were unequally yoked.

Ruth was a Moabite, a people who were expected to lose their virginity as prostitutes of Baal. We don't know about her early life before her marriage to Kilion. Boaz was a Jewish man from the tribe of Judah and an heir of Abraham. He married a woman many would not have approved of, yet he never hesitated. When he saw Ruth for the first time, he took an interest and began to find out about her soul, virtue, and values. He didn't care how rich she was or how dark she wasn't. He had enough money for the both of them and was more concerned about her values than her body or face.

He might have been actively looking for his right woman for years, but the Lord hadn't brought her. Within seven weeks of meeting Ruth, he knew she was the one. The number seven is symbolic of completion, finished work, perfection in the spirit, and rest. Boaz did not allow the shallowness of the world to cloud his judgment, regardless of Ruth's past or the visibility that would eventually fade.

If you can open your heart, travel to a place with God, look through the baggage, and do your research on a woman's values and beliefs, you might have your girl. But you might be so concerned about the things that don't really matter—those things that are shallow to the heart—that you might miss her. Boaz knew he had a woman of value and took claim of her.

Do you know your Ruth? Have you claimed her? When our other halves arrive, we will be complete. The ultimate testimony to the importance of marriage was the birth of our Lord and Savior Jesus Christ. Ruth and Boaz were two of the greatest examples of the faithfulness of God in the genealogy of Christ in all human history.

A Message from Tee Ashira

If you have a Boaz now, celebrate with him. Let his joys be your joys, and let his sorrows be your prayers. We must not allow our fathers' absence and the abuse from the previous affairs of the heart make us bitter and loathe submission because of the bad example of authority that was placed over us. We must be like Ruth and let go of the sorrows of yesterday. Arise, your Boaz is approaching; and even though he has not arrived yet, allow God to continue a good work in you.

To all the women who have experienced this same pain, you might have thought you had a David—a man after God's own heart—but the truth is that the devil is a deceiver. That is his job. Today I plead the blood of Jesus over you, as it was pleaded over me, that you have the strength to walk away because when our God gives, he gives with no sorrow. Will the fists and the emotional abuse continue into your daughter's life? You are her foundation. What you accept, she will also think is acceptable. You have paid the price emotionally, physically, and spiritually. I must also remind you that you are paying a double debt because Christ came to take on all of your pain, so why suffer twice? And for the men who have brought any means of abuse on a woman— physically, mentally or spiritually—you might think that this behavior is normal, but I assure you that the seeds you sow will reap a poor harvest. Only God can reveal the sins of a man to his heart. I know that the mother who might have been absent emotionally or physically has left you in a mess.

I must refresh your heart and tell you that God is in the business of cleaning up messes. For every woman who has hurt you, I say from the God that resides in me, I'm sorry. I wish I could restore the entire loss or losses in the past that you have suffered, those that your mother or any other woman was trusted to restore in you. I can't, but I know a God who can. Allow him to heal you in these areas, and then we can surely rejoice because we will raise kings who will treat our women like queens. Teach your sons to respect God and have an intimate relationship with him so they can be men after God's own heart and men truly to be admired. Raise each one to be a Boaz; he learned this greatness from his father, and your daughter won't marry anything less than what you allowed God to place in you. For married couples who think that their marriage is dead, you must know that nothing is beyond God's repair. When God looked at David, he did not see a small shepherd boy. He saw a king who would rule Israel. When God saw Simon—the fisherman, coward, and betrayer who would later be renamed Peter—he saw the first apostle of Jesus. When God looked at Solomon, he did not see an idol worshipper; he saw an architect, a man who would build the temple of God and be the third king of Israel. Although these men had flaws in their characters, God saw the greatness in all of them and saw what they would become, not what they were.

When God looked at me, he did not see a divorcée or a woman scorned, molested, hurt, and rejected at a young age. When God looked at me, he did not see a former *Playboy* model. No, he saw a little girl from Mississippi—a mother, wife, friend, and entrepreneur—through whom he would later birth a ministry. He saw a young woman he would redeem when there was no earthly redeemer present. He saw the Boaz that he had prepared for me, who also spent years waiting for his wife—a man who was groomed for me by God's heart and hands, who would be submissive to the will of God for his life, and who could have chosen many but was ordained to choose me.

When God looked at Ruth, he did not see a Moabite girl who lost her virginity to Baal. No, he saw a woman of virtue who would later be redeemed. He saw the wife of Boaz and the great-grandmother of King David. Do not allow the memories of yesterday to leave you in bondage. Babylon is unclean to you; allow God to remove the former pains from your mind—the pains of addictions, molestations, or any type of other abuse you might have endured. But until this happens for you, the redeemer is ready to redeem you. He has arrived.

God's Dwelling Place

There are phases of the planting process called seed time and harvest time. We plant the seed and wait for the harvest. We should sow seeds in our prayers for our Boaz or Ruth.

If you have prayed that prayer for years and the gift has not yet arrived, maybe God is saying, "Wait, my child. There is still a work to be done in you." What people fail to realize is that we need to spend more time allowing God to heal our inner selves before we get the gift of the other half. If you are broken before your mate arrives, you will be broken with your mate. Love God and yourself first, before that person arrives, and then you can love that man or woman naturally. Take your focus off of the physical and pray in the spiritual for your mate before he or she arrives because, in the end, all else will fade, but the spiritual is God's dwelling place.

Ruth: The Symbolic Message

The story of Ruth is the vindication of the concept of a marriage culture. Through it, we can see how the Lord overcomes every obstacle to fulfill his promises to mankind and how the plan of God provides great order in marriage. Ruth is a symbol for God's rewards for faithfulness. Seek him with vengeance while he can be found so you can give to your daughters what was not given to you. And because your sons will have a role model to live up to, they won't have to search for that acceptance in the world.

Acceptance at the Throne

I want to always give my readers who do not know God a chance to establish a personal relationship with him. We need to know the importance of that relationship with the Almighty or we cannot start the process of becoming as great as Ruth and Boaz.

Romans 10:9–11

> If you confess with your mouth that Jesus is lord and believe in your heart that God rose him from the dead, you will be saved. For it is by believing in your heart that you are

made right with God, and it is by confessing with your mouth that you are saved. As the Scriptures tell us, "Anyone who trusts in him will not be disgraced."

Please repeat this prayer my friend: "Lord Jesus, I confess that I am a sinner. Please forgive me for my sins. I receive you as my lord and savior. I believe that you are the Son of God. Thank you for healing my past. I come before you and ask that you to wash me clean as snow so that I can begin the process of becoming a Boaz or a Ruth in spirit, body, and mind. In Jesus I pray, amen."

Now that we stand healed, I know what you're saying, Okay, Tee Austin, did you find your Boaz? You better believe that the master himself handcrafted my man from the day that he was born for me and me alone. No matter what the circumstances were in my past, my future was designed by God. I followed God's purpose for my life. You are my purpose. Your healing is my desire.

No, my dear friends, I did not find my Boaz. My Boaz found me.

Seven Days of Completion Prayer

I want you to take the next seven days, regardless of whether you are single or married, to clean up the areas needed to become that Boaz or Ruth. And I want you to trust a God you may not know and cannot see.

Day One

The number one is symbolic of new beginnings, unity, and order.

Lord, today is a day that I set my heart on recognizing all the areas in my life in which new, positive thoughts and order must take place.

Day Two

Two is symbolic of separation, discernment, and dividing light from darkness.

Lord, allow your spirit to penetrate me to the struggles in my heart that would separate me from you and my spiritual mate.

Day Three

Three is symbolic of divine fullness, solid attributes, conformity, resurrection, power over sin, the godhead, and the Trinity.

Lord, I thank you for your resurrection power, and I realize that you are the head of my life. I have victory and power over all the battles that I may face or have already faced.

Day Four

Four is symbolic of the world, earth, work, and creation.

Father, I thank you that today I admire your creation and that I am faced with the challenge of the work you have set out for me today. I stand in submission to my calling for whomever or whatever you have for me. I am patient and willing to endure the trials and temptations of being single and of the happiness of a covenant partner that you have placed or will place in my life.

Day Five

Five is symbolic of grace and completion.

Lord, grant me grace and completeness in every way. Grant the partner that you have for me with the same grace and completeness.

Day Six

The number six is symbolic of secular completeness, Satan, and sorrow.

Father, you have given me power over the enemy to defeat him in all my battles today, and I realize that I must be complete in my spirit and that there are secular ways I must part with. Knowing that I can do all things through Christ Jesus, I am prepared for all quests against sorrow, Satan, and a secular life. I thank you for the conquering power of completeness.

Day Seven

Seven is symbolic of completion, finished work, and rest in the spirit.

Father, I thank you that, before I note in my diary today, I rejoice in my transformation, and I rest in spirit knowing that my Boaz has entered in spirit or in body. I thank you that I remain holy and in virtue. I thank you for all the great things that I have left at the threshing floor; the pains of the past are gone. Allow me to start my life with this person, whether it be you or the Boaz that you have set before me, at full throttle and give you the praise in all my victories for many years to come.

Amen.

Today is a new day after day seven, so start thanking God now. If you are still married to the Boaz that you might already possess and have taken it for granted, repent and move into happiness. If you and your spouse are not walking in the calling of a Boaz or Ruth, believe God that the time for transformation is now! And if you are a woman waiting for that Boaz to enter, your wait is not in vain. Start thanking God every day until your Boaz arrives in the spirit because I assure you that he will manifest in the physical. That's the power of God.

Day Eight

(Make special notes about your personal transformation before your mate arrives.)

Your Boaz

What values do you want him to possess?

Dear Diary,

Dear Diary,

Dear Diary,

Dear Diary,

Dear Diary,

Dear Diary,

Dear Diary,

Scriptures for the Woman Who Awaits Her Boaz

Scriptures

Scriptures

Scriptures

Scriptures

Meditation Scriptures

Meditation Scriptures

Meditation Scriptures

Meditation Scriptures

Notes

Picture of Boaz